Something

Wicked

Sarah Dale

For Jennifer and Sue

For showing me a larger world and how to live in it

Printed in the United States of America

First edition published, 2018

This edition Printed, 2019

ISBN-13: 978-1-948661-58-4
AISN: 978-1-948661-57-7

If you're reading this, you've found my hidey hole. I've been keeping journals of our adventures for more than three decades now, and up until last week, I believed them to be safely hidden in my home. Now, everything has changed.

It's not that I fear they will be discovered, rather the opposite. I fear they'll be destroyed, and the record of our life's work would simply disappear.

I'm putting them here for safekeeping. I've spent enough hours in this library to know what gets tended regularly, and what gets regularly overlooked. So if you're finding this now, you must be doing a deep clean, or maybe, just maybe, the City has come together with the funds for a new building, and this one is being cleared out.

Do me a favor. Do what you can to keep these safe. Tuck them back away, or move them if you need to, but don't let them be destroyed.

And if it's you they're meant for, then, good luck, my friend. You're going to need it.

I don't really know if I should be doing this, writing everything down. Mr. Rakow always said that since not everyone is able to see the evils we battle, being transparent about what we do would turn into a massive legal, moral and political disaster. I've always agreed with this assessment. I absolutely understand the importance of our work, and the chaos that would result if there weren't people like us who are freely able to fight on the front lines.

But, what about the future? Won't our experiences help the next 'Cuspers' or 'soldiers' or whatever they call themselves? As far as I'm concerned, they're going to need all the help they can get. The bad guys, the angry ghosts, the demons, the monsters — they aren't ever going to quit coming at us.

So I'm writing it down. I'm compiling the notes and scribbles from my journals into a passably coherent narrative, in the hopes that it can be used to help future demon fighters.

But I can't pretend that's all of it.

This is our story. This was our childhood. These are the things that shaped us, me and Jenny and David, into the adults we became. I don't know if it makes us heroes, or crazy, or outlaws or what, but it's our story, and it's up to me to tell it.

So here goes.

My name is Angie Parsons. My best friends were, and always will be, Jennifer Howe and David Owens. The summer before junior high, the three of us were forcibly indoctrinated into a part of our world that stays unseen by most, but not all people. Some of us can see. Some of us can't help but see.

We were lucky. Mr. Rakow was already looking out for us, and when it happened, he was there to help. He and Jenny's mom, Lorraine, showed us what we could do, helped us learn our strengths. They helped us not only survive, but taught us how to help other people, too.

It changed us, of course. We grew up in a secret war zone. We had to face truths other kids didn't. At the same time, we were stuck facing the truths every kid does. From zits to zombies, even the luckiest kid doesn't get through junior high and high school unscathed. Our job added a little extra life-threatening danger to the whole thing.

Ok, maybe a lot.

There were plenty of times we wanted to quit. Just back out of the whole mess and be normal. I realize now, a whole lot of what I wrote in these journals was my struggle to determine what kind of a person I am, and why I was making these – sometimes spectacularly stupid – life choices.

The journey isn't over yet, so I can't tell you how it ends. But this is how it begins.

"By the pricking of my thumbs, something wicked
this way comes."
Macbeth

I couldn't remember a time before Jenny, David and
I were best friends. I know David's mom didn't move
here until halfway through our kindergarten year, but I
don't remember that part of it. He was always just there,
with Jenny and me, running around at recess, walking
home from school, spending summers at the swimming
pool. The three of us.

David had some guy friends, too, including Jen's
twin brother, Jon, but they weren't best friends the way
the three of us were. We never thought it was weird, that
David's best friends were two girls; and back then, I don't
remember anybody else getting too bent out of shape
about it either. I think most of his guy friends were a little
jealous. None of them could get girls to give them the
time of day, usually.

Both David and Jenny lived with their moms.
Their dads weren't really in the picture much. Jenny's dad
would show up occasionally, mostly during the summer,
and maybe stay a few days. Sometimes he'd take us all out
for burgers or bring home a bucket of chicken, and we'd
all eat at the picnic table in Jen's backyard. Her dad always
got enough for everybody, including David and me, plus
Jen's twin brother Jon, and his friends. But David's dad
never came around, and David never talked about him.

Back then, I was the out-of-the-ordinary one. I
think I was one of two or three kids on our whole street
whose parents weren't divorced.

I sure don't remember Jenny's mom ever bringing
boyfriends around. I think she went on dates sometimes.
I know there were times Jen would spend the night because her mom was going to the movies, but there wasn't
ever anybody serious. David's mom was different.

There was a string of boyfriends for his mom. None

of them hung around long. Often, I didn't even know a name, just a car. There was green Chevelle guy, El Camino guy, crappy gold Duster guy, there was even a motorcycle guy or two, but no names. Nobody memorable anyway, until Mitch. Mitch showed up about the beginning of sixth grade, and he stuck around. It wasn't too long after he showed up that things started to change.

Jenny's house was normally the hangout house. My folks didn't allow my sister and me to have more than one friend each come over after school. They both worked so we were on our own until they got home. We never hung out at David's. Jen's mom didn't care if we came to their house, as long as we didn't mess stuff up too bad. She kept a huge stockpile of cheap store-brand pop in the basement fridge, and we were allowed to make as much popcorn as we could eat in the air popper. It was the fall of 1982 when we started sixth grade. Some people had microwaves. Jen's mom had considered it but opted instead for paying extra to get MTV. We all worshiped her for her wisdom in this.

There were usually six or seven of us at Jen and Jon's house after school. If it was nice, we'd get a snack and then head outside. Jenny's house was on a block that once upon a time had a trolley car track running through it. The trolley cars were long gone, and even the tracks had been removed, but the city never sold the land. So, for a mile or so between our neighborhood and downtown, there was a wide grassy space between the houses in the middle of the block, and we kids took full advantage.

We played touch football, softball, staged gymnastics contests, ran races, played freeze tag, hide and seek, whatever we could think up that required almost no equipment and that most of us could agree on for at least one or maybe two afternoons in a row. I sucked at most sports, but nobody really cared. Jenny and David had an ongoing bet to see who could run the fastest from the sidewalk at one end of the block all the way to the sidewalk at the other end. He was a little faster; she had longer legs. Sometimes he would win, sometimes she would, most often they tied. I was either the start or the finish line ref. They raced each other two or three times a week for years, up until that summer of '83.

Most Friday nights, sometimes Saturdays too, and even more often during the summer, a bunch of us would end up spending the night at Jen and Jon's. They didn't have a super big house or anything, but they had a big basement with a couple of giant, old, beat-up couches and a big TV. Jon's room was downstairs, Jen's was up, next to her mom's, but usually, we all just crashed out on the couches or the floor downstairs. None of Jon's friends ever bothered Jenny or me, probably because they knew they'd get the crap beat out of them if they tried anything. Jon and David were pretty protective of us; but the truth was, Jen was the real badass. Nobody dared tangle with Jen.

Things started to get bad for David after Christmas break in sixth grade. I remember we were all busy with family stuff and didn't see much of each other over break. When we got back to school in January, something was different.

David was a fun guy. He was always cracking jokes and playing pranks on the rest of us. It was all good-natured stuff, salt in somebody's iced tea, a closet full of balloons, and of course, after we all saw *Caddyshack*, there was the occasional Baby Ruth floater. Classics. But after Christmas that year, something was different. Jenny and I noticed it right away and tried to get him to talk, but he wouldn't.

It was sometime around Valentine's Day that he first showed up at school with bruises on his wrists. Not long after that, one of the first days when the weather was nice enough to wear shorts, we saw the burns on his legs. Jen got really worried when she saw that. Nobody at my house smoked cigarettes, so when I saw the pattern on the back of his left calf, I didn't click on it right away. Jenny did. She told her mom.

After that, David started sleeping over at Jen's house every single weekend, and even some school nights, too.

Summer vacation couldn't come fast enough for any of us. It was one of those years in which we'd used up so many snow days during the winter that we had to make up days. That meant, here we were now in the second week of June and still in school. Even the teachers were fading.

We'd put a good deal of planning into the first sleepover of the summer. Last Halloween, we'd had to come up with a contingency plan, because it looked like we were going to have a snowstorm that night and weren't going to be able to trick or treat. We'd put our heads together and come up with a list of scary movies we wanted to watch if we had to stay in. We'd lucked out, and the weather had held, but we hadn't given up on our horror movie night. A couple of new ones had come out since October too, that we were all hot to see; so that was the big plan. Halloween in summer. Horror movie fiesta extraordinaire.

Plus, that spring, Jen had finally talked her mom into letting her get a paper route. Back then, there weren't many options for kids our age to make extra money, but paper routes were a good gig if you could get them. As luck would have it, the kid who had the one right in our neighborhood was looking to give his up. Jen had had to do some fast talking to get her mom to agree to let her take it. You had to get up at like five in the morning and go out in the dark, get the papers, fold them, deliver the whole route which was usually about an hour, forty-five minutes maybe if you had a good bike, and then get home in time to get ready for school.

The kid who was giving up the route wanted to have it covered before Memorial Day weekend. He had some big trip planned with his scout troop, so he wanted somebody who could take over a few weeks before the end of the school year. That first week, he went with her every morning, and then she was on her own. I'd never seen Jenny really exhausted at school before that, but she stuck to it. By the time school was out, she was more or less used to her new schedule.

Finally, the last day of school arrived. It was our last day of elementary school, too. Next year would be junior high. There was a picnic, and we were given a field day afternoon of games and free time. It was a pretty awesome day. Near the end, when we were all gathering in the shade, and the teachers were counting heads, Jenny, David and I were huddled together discussing plans for our evening.

"My mom's renting the movies tonight," Jen said, lifting one strap of her tank top and examining her potential sunburn. "It's a good thing she went in last week to make sure they had them all, too. They had to put her on the waiting list for *Creepshow* and *Poltergeist*."

"Of course, *Creepshow* would be the one Jon and those guys would be all psyched to see. That's gonna be the gross-out one," I said, trying to let disdain mask my nervousness. I liked scary movies, but the blood and gore kind of freaked me out.

"Don't worry, Angie," David said in a stage whisper. He gave me a friendly shoulder bump. "I'll sit in front of you on the couch again so you can hide your eyes, and Matt and Terry won't see and give you a hard time."

"And if they do give you a hard time," Jenny interjected, "I'll kill them."

I sighed happily. "You guys are totally awesome. I'm stoked about seeing *Something Wicked This Way Comes*, the book was so frickin' good." I was the book nerd of the three of us. I could sometimes get Jenny to read some book I was excited about, but we'd always have to give David the *Reader's Digest Condensed* version afterward. He was way too active to spend much time sitting around reading.

"Yeah, it sounds pretty cool," David said. He was bouncing lightly on the balls of his feet, looking over at the teachers. They were just returning from extricating a group of wasteoids from the covered top of the tornado slide where they were probably smoking a joint. "What was the one your mom and her friend wanted to see, Jenny?"

"Um, Werewolf something. *American Werewolf in London*."

"Oh yeah, that's the one with the really cool special effects." David was a movie freak. He and Jon, both. They'd see just about anything, but they were partial to the science fiction stuff. We'd all seen the *Star Wars* movies by then, of course, but Jon and David were obsessed.

"Did you know…" David began in his *I'm about to drop an amazing piece of trivia on you guys* voice. Jenny and I glanced at each other and hid smiles. "Did you know that the guy who did the special werewolf makeup for *American Werewolf in London*, Rick Baker, worked on the set of the first *Star Wars* movie? He was on the makeup team, but he's also in the Cantina scene. He plays Figrin D'an, the sort of light-bulb-headed guy playing the thing that looks like – what's that instrument you want to play next year, Ang?"

"The oboe," I replied.

"Yeah. He plays a thing that looks like an oboe made out of a giant spark plug." I had a pretty good recollection of the guy he meant, given how many times we'd seen that first *Star Wars* movie by now. *Return of the Jedi* had only been out a couple of weeks, and David and Jon had already seen it four times. Any time any of the theaters would replay one or all of the movies on a slow day, they had to go; and the year before when they'd finally come out on VHS, the guys figured out how to copy the tapes from one VCR to another and made themselves illegal bootlegs. We'd watched those so many times they were practically worn out.

Jenny and I rolled our eyes at him at the exact same time and grinned. "Whaaaaat?" he drawled, acting like we were the crazy ones for not being as geeked about the whole thing as he was. It was dumb, but we made each other laugh.

The teachers finally got everybody together, and we were herded back up the hill to the school so we could clean out our lockers before the 3:00 bell.

"Oh, hey David," Jen said, "I just remembered. Your mom called last night and said you should stop home and get clean clothes and stuff."

David's face fell. My heart felt abruptly cold in my chest. He still wasn't talking about what was going on at home with his mom and her boyfriend Mitch. I knew Jenny's mom and his mom had talked, and that David's mom was okay with him spending so much time over at her house, but he had to go home sometimes. The few times I'd been around when his mom called, I'd tried to read the expression on his face. It was like he was fighting a war inside his head when he talked to her. He loved his mom, and he was super protective of her, but I think he was mad at her too, for being such a mess.

I couldn't imagine what it would be like to have a mom that got drunk a lot and smoked cigarettes and came outside in her nightgown. My mom was, like, the complete opposite. She worked in the administration office at a big hospital and always dressed nice and was super smart. She'd started going back to school last year, trying to finish the degree she had begun before my sister and I entered the picture. Jenny's mom was way more rad than mine, sometimes she drank wine coolers; and once or twice, when her friend Wanda came over, we were pretty sure we smelled pot. But she was also totally with it. She had a good job and the house was always pretty clean, considering how many kids were running around all the time.

David's house was always a maze of dirty dishes and full ashtrays; and now, with Mitch there, the driveway was always filled with some car he was fixing up and boxes of crap he brought home from someplace. Their front yard got mowed when the neighbors threatened to call the city, but the backyard was a jungle. I didn't know how David could even bear to be there a few days a week.

"We'll walk over with you on the way home. It'll only take a sec, right?" I asked, trying to sound cheerful.

"It'll be cool," Jen interjected. "My mom told your mom she needed us to all be at my house by 4:00 because she needs us to help her get stuff ready for tonight."

"You guys don't have to come with me. I can just meet you at Jen's," he muttered.

"Don't be dumb," Jen said, simply. "This is us, remember? We stick together like always."

We walked on in silence for a while. I don't know what the others were thinking, but I was hoping Mitch wouldn't be home.

He gave me the creeps. He treated me differently than Jenny. Jen was tall and strong. She was the tallest kid in sixth grade, not the tallest girl, the tallest kid. She even topped her twin by about half an inch, which he hated, of course. She was taller than some of the teachers. And she was tough. I'd watched her stand down kids on the playground starting in first grade.

I was neither tall nor strong. I was little and clumsy. Nobody in my family played sports. We all wore thick glasses and played obscure orchestra instruments. That made me fair game for all kinds of jerks, and so far; Mitch was the worst one. I crossed my fingers that he'd be gone.

It didn't work.

Not only was he home when we got there, but he was awake, and he'd been drinking. There was one lone beer can sitting on the trunk of the car he was working on. It was still attached to the plastic rings that held the six-pack together.

"Hey, kids!" Mitch drawled, grinning, as he watched us approach. He had on trashed jeans and no shirt. His greasy hair was pulled back in a ponytail. There was a badly drawn tattoo on his skinny chest. David told me it was supposed to be the cover art from Iron Maiden's first album, but it ended up looking more like an angry green troll doll.

"Last day of school, huh? Y'all ready for a good long summer?" He drew out the words *good* and *long*, staring right at me as he said them. I cringed. I wasn't even sure why what he was saying sounded so bad, but his tone and the look on his face made me feel dirty and exposed.

Jenny must have understood him, though, because she stiffened and stepped ahead of me, partially blocking me from Mitch's view. I couldn't see the expression on her face, but I'm sure it was fierce. He shifted his gaze from me to Jen and then found someplace easier to look. Unfortunately, that left David.

"Hey there, little buddy." He greeted David with a punch to the shoulder that was far from playful. David didn't flinch, but the force of the blow spun him around. The three of us were attempting to make a beeline for the gate leading to the backyard. We always went in through the back door, that way we could duck directly downstairs to his basement bedroom and bypass the rest of the house.

"Where do you think you're going?" Mitch's voice was mocking and cruel. "Gonna take your girlfriends down to your bedroom? Gonna get it on?"

"Shut up, Mitch." David's voice was low and a little uncertain, but there was no doubt in my mind that he was furious.

"Ah, no, you wouldn't do that, would you, Davey? 'Cause that's not how you are, are you? Nah, Davey doesn't like girls, now does he?"

"Shut up, Mitch." David's voice was louder this time.

Mitch took hold of the collar of David's t-shirt. He twisted it in his greasy fist. The shirt was yellow, and it had Han and Chewie charging out, weapons blazing, surrounded by a silver box, and the *Star Wars* logo kind of diagonally across the top. It was one of his very favorites. He'd bought it with money he earned himself, painting fences and doing odd jobs for his neighbor. Mitch pulled David a step or two away from us but still close enough that we could hear him clearly.

He leaned down close to David's face, and in a low, nasty voice said, "Maybe I ought to come down there with you, show you what a man is supposed to act like." Then he laughed, casting his eyes over to where I was standing, frozen, next to Jenny at the edge of the driveway. "What do you say to that, pretty Angie?" He didn't say my name so much as he sang it, like that Rolling Stones song.

"Or maybe," Jenny growled, taking a step toward Mitch, "maybe you ought to do just what David said and *shut the hell up, Mitch!*"

Mitch's dull eyes widened just then, but he wasn't looking at Jenny. I heard a screen door slam at the house next door, and Mr. Rakow came outside. He leaned on his porch railing and called over, "Hey kids, hey Mitch. Everything okay over there?"

Mr. Rakow was a good guy if a little strange. My dad said he'd been in Vietnam and that was hard on everybody. Sometimes he still wore his US Army t-shirts and he had an awful lot of tattoos. He also had a huge German Shepherd named Shadow. The dog adored us kids, but right now he was poised, looking at Mitch like he was just waiting for permission from Mr. Rakow to explode off the porch and consume him whole.

"Hey, Mr. Rakow!" I called. My voice sounded a little funny. "Hey, Shadow!" Shadow's tail wagged at the sound of my voice, but he never took his eyes off Mitch.

Mitch's fingers uncurled from David's t-shirt. He nodded curtly at the neighbor and gave David's shoulder a squeeze. "Hey man, how's tricks?"

David shrugged angrily and very deliberately turned his back on Mitch. He walked calmly over to stand next to Jenny and me, smiled and said, "Hey, Mr. Rakow." We all moved over closer to Mr. Rakow's porch.

"Hey, David." He made a nearly imperceptible motion with one hand, and Shadow relaxed. Another slight hand movement and Shadow sat, grinning happily at us with his tongue hanging out. "You planning on coming out to the range with me again sometime? I have some new pistols you might like to try out." I noticed he raised his voice a little as he said this, making sure Mitch heard.

"Yeah!" David replied happily. "I asked my mom, and she's cool with it. Just let me know when you're going."

"Will do, kid. Now, go on, do your business and get out of here. That damn fool over there ain't got no good in him today. Not that he ever does. You all goin' back over to Miss Jenny's?"

"Yeah," David answered, and we nodded assent.

"Good. Jenny, you tell your mama I've got my eye on things here. Now go on, *di di mau*."

"Yes, sir!" David grinned.

"Don't you be callin' me sir! I ain't no officer!" Mr. Rakow looked around quickly, as though someone might hear. Shadow moved a little closer to him, and I could see him visibly relax when he felt the dog touch his leg.

"No, sorry. We're going. We'll just be a sec," David stumbled over his words a little. Jenny already had the back gate unlocked, and we hurried through. Mr. Rakow was great, but he could be a little spooky in his own way. It was time for us to go.

We zipped through the back door and down to David's room. Unlike the semi-squalor of the rest of the house, his room was a haven of neatness. His bed was always made, his desk was always straightened up, and he always put away his clothes. The posters on the walls were all precisely even, like in a museum. I couldn't compete. Much as I tried, my room always looked like a tribe of excited goats had just passed through.

David emptied the contents of his backpack onto his desk, put pens in the pen can, tossed a few worksheets in the trash, put a book on the shelf, and then proceeded to fill the pack with clean clothes. Jen and I perched on the edge of his bed. We didn't wait long. Five minutes tops and we were headed back up the stairs.

Halfway to the top, a shadow fell over us. Mitch was

blocking our exit.

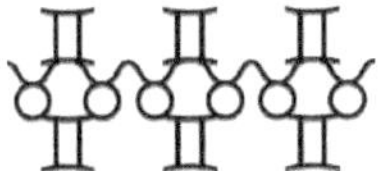

David had gone up first; I was behind him, and Jen was behind me. David paused, briefly. "What do you want, Mitch?" His voice was sour.

"Your mama wants to talk to you, Davey," Mitch sneered.

David pushed past him clearing a path for me and continued through the kitchen into the living room, where his mom was sitting.

I tried to skirt around Mitch into the kitchen, but I wasn't quite fast enough to avoid his hand. I cringed as his cold fingertips touched my hip and trailed down to where my shorts gave way to bare leg. I swatted at his hand like I would a bug. A slimy, nasty, million-legged bug. He started to laugh, but it turned into a gasp.

Jenny was right behind me. She saw the whole thing. She bounded up the last step and strode into the kitchen her arms bent as if she were running a race. When she passed Mitch, one of her hands crossed his back, and a long red scratch appeared.

"What the…" he shouted, turning and reaching for his back.

"Oh, hell, Mitch, sorry about that! Must have caught you with my ring here," she said, flashing the tiny birth-stone ring she wore on her pinky. He stopped looking over his shoulder trying to see the damage long enough to lunge at Jen, who was anticipating it. She never stopped moving and pushed me along with her into the living room. Mitch restrained himself before David's mom could see anything.

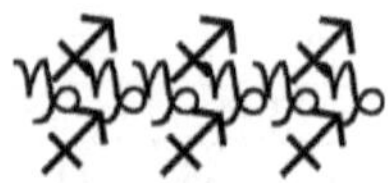

"Hey, Donna," Jen greeted David's mom cheerily. His mom always insisted we call her by her first name.

Donna smiled vacantly. "Hi, Jenny honey. Hello Angel." She always called me Angel. "You guys got big plans for tonight?"

"Movie marathon," I responded.

"You kids and your movies. That's all this one talks about," she said, fondly ruffling David's hair. His expression was a cross between embarrassment and sadness. "Well, I think Mitch and I are going out tonight, too. There's a band playing, who is it, honey?"

"Unholy Sins," announced Mitch from the kitchen doorway.

"That's right," said Donna. "Mitch's friend Steve is in the band."

"Steve Ryan?" David asked, surprised. "Wasn't he the guy who died last fall?"

"Nope!" crowed Mitch. "Ain't nothing can kill that motherfucker." He crushed his beer can and tossed it in the general direction of the kitchen trash. "If something tried, he'd probably kick the devil in the teeth and come right back anyway!" He seemed delighted by this idea.

"Well, be careful, Mom." David leaned in for a hug. "I'll call you tomorrow, okay?"

Donna moved her lit cigarette out of the way just enough to hug David without lighting his hair on fire. "Okay, honey. I love you." She sounded worn out.

"Love you too," he replied, standing. Jen pushed open the screen door, and the three of us headed outside.

We'd just made it to the sidewalk when we heard Mitch's voice from the porch.

"How's that paper route going for you, Jenny? Kinda dark and scary out there in the mornings, ain't it?" Mitch wiped his chin with the back of his hand and showed us his rotten teeth in a grin.

"Whatever," shrugged Jen.

"You should be careful, little girl. These two ain't no kind of protection. Angie's just a sweet little thing, and Davey is, well, now Davey's just a sweet little thing, too, ain't he?" The leer on Mitch's face was horrible. The hairs stood up on the back of my neck. He freaked me out so bad. I just wanted away from there, but Jenny and David had stopped and turned back toward him, so I had to stop too.

Out of the corner of my eye, I saw Mr. Rakow's screen door flash open. Mitch continued, unaware. "Can't count on Davey, he's too little to stand up for himself, no matter how much he wants to protect his girlfriends. He's just a little pussy faggot hisself, aren't you, Daaa…."

His words cut off like a switch when he saw Shadow bolting full speed across the lawn, straight towards him. He jumped backward, scrambling to catch hold of the screen door, cursing loudly. He was mostly inside before Shadow hit it, smashing his leg between the door and the door frame.

Shadow, who had been completely silent as he rushed the house, broke into a series of short, harsh barks. He didn't try to bite Mitch, all he did was make sure he went inside and didn't come back out. We could hear Mitch cussing from inside, even over the barking, and Mr. Rakow's explosive laughter.

Jenny whooped, and David let out a shout. It was all I could do to breathe in and out and not pee my pants. I was sure we would all laugh about it later, but right now, I was just totally wigged out.

"Screw you, Mitch!" Jenny crowed, laughing and hooting. Mr. Rakow had walked out to the sidewalk to stand with us. As soon as he saw the screen door was completely closed, he called to Shadow, who came promptly and sat, tongue hanging out, at his master's feet. He happily accepted our lavish praise and ear scritches.

"C'mon, kids. I'll walk you to the corner." Mr. Rakow walked with a limp, but he wasn't slow. He shepherded us along in front of him, in the direction of Jenny's house. Shadow trotted alongside, tail wagging. David kept looking back over his shoulder.

"Don't worry about your mom, kid. Me and Shadow, we've got her six. Always have."

"I know, Mr. Rakow. Thanks." David sounded miserable, but angry too.

"You kids get on home now. You doing that paper route together in the morning, are you?"

"That's the plan," I offered.

"Start out at zero five hundred hours?" he asked.

"About then," Jenny replied, turning to look at Mr. Rakow. "I wouldn't worry about him in the morning, though. He'll be so damn hungover; he won't know his ass from his elbow." That was one of Jenny's mom's favorite sayings.

"Likely so, Miss Jen. You kids keep a sharp eye out just the same, all right?" By this time, we were more than a block from David's house, about to round the corner.

"Will do," Jen nodded.

"And David," Mr. Rakow took him by the shoulder. "I think you know this already, but that man is a damfool. I've seen some cowards in my time, and plenty of fine men, too. You got a brave heart, kid, and even though that pile of shit is bigger than you are right now, he's a coward. He's got nothing on you."

David didn't smile, exactly, but his expression lightened a little.

"Cowards can be dangerous, but you already know that. He ain't brave enough to come at a fight face-to-face, but you all need to watch your backs and look out for each other. Don't let that little shit pull anything sneaky. Y'all hear me?"

"Yeah," we all chimed in.

He was right. Whatever Mitch had done to David, and I was sure he had done stuff that I didn't know about, whatever it was must have been sneaky and underhanded. He wasn't a big guy, and David was no pushover. He might not be big enough to take Mitch down in a fight, but he was strong and athletic. He would be hard to pin down if he was determined to fight back. Whatever Mitch was doing; it must be sneaky shit.

So, we just had to be smart. I might not be good at a lot of stuff, but I was pretty good at being smart. This was just a new problem that needed solving. We left Mr. Rakow and Shadow at the corner and took off for Jen's house. I'd dropped my backpack off there that morning, so I didn't even have to go home to get anything. Jen's mom was supposed to get off work early, so we could go pick up the movies from the rental place. It was going to be a great night.

It was 4:30 in the morning before the last movie ended. We'd watched *Poltergeist* first, and then *Creepshow*, which was exactly as horrifying as I'd feared. The cockroach thing still had me twitchy. *American Werewolf* was awesome; the special effects were every bit as amazing as

David promised. The scene where he changes into a werewolf for the first time, we actually rewound the tape and watched it twice, it was that cool. And *Something Wicked This Way Comes* did a pretty amazing job of being as eerie and creepy as the book.

Jen's mom, and her friend Wanda, had gone upstairs a while before, and Jon and his friends were passed out asleep on the floor. We tiptoed between the sprawled, sleeping bodies and crept upstairs. We found our shoes, and Jen hung her house key around her neck. The van bearing the bundles of newspapers got to Jen's pickup corner just before 5:00 a.m. With the three of us, we might be done and be back home before 6:00. I was no pro at staying up all night. I'd done it a couple of times at sleepovers, but after a full day of school and running around, I was about done for.

David grabbed Jen's newspaper bag, and we filed out the door. When I saw how dark it still was, I asked, "Should we take the flashlight?"

"Sure, if you want to carry it. Mom puts it there by the door for me, but I don't always feel like packing it along. Damn thing's heavy." I hefted the big light. It was one like cops use, the kind that takes four of the big D-cell batteries. I liked the way it felt in my hand. She was right, it was heavy, but I took it anyway.

We started the four-block walk down to the corner where we'd pick up the papers in relative quiet. Everyone was tired. The movement energized us, though; and by the time we got to the corner, we were comparing notes about which movie we'd liked best.

"*Creepshow* was good, but it's like, kinda old-timey," David said.

"Yeah, those comic books were around even before Mom's time," Jen said. "She told me her uncle Joe had some old ones in his room at Grandma's house, and they totally freaked her out. She and her sister would dare each other to go in there and look at them."

"I think some of those comics had stories in them by the same guy who wrote *Something Wicked*" David mused.

"Bradbury? Really?" I asked, my attention piqued.

"Yeah, pretty sure they did some of his stories. I saw some one time when you guys dragged me to the library sale, downtown."

"Cool!" I wondered if my favorite librarian could find some of those for me. Creepy as they were, I loved the idea of Bradbury stories in comic form. I'd have to remember to ask her next time I was there.

We arrived at the corner just as two fat bundles of newspapers were being tossed out of the blue van. Jen raised one hand to the driver, who saluted and went on his way.

Jen took a retractable box cutter from her jeans pocket and popped the plastic band off the stack of papers. The three of us sat, cross-legged on the sidewalk and folded papers and rubber-banded them. It was a Thursday morning, which meant it was ads day. Sundays were the worst, Jen said, but Thursday's papers were pretty huge with all the extra pages stuck in the middle. We made an assembly line, David forcing the paper to fold into thirds, Jen wrapping the rubber band around each and me organizing them as evenly as possible into the bags.

The bags were designed to be worn over your head, with big pockets hanging both front and back. Some kids wrapped them over the handlebars of their bikes, instead. Fully loaded with Thursday papers, the thing weighed a ton.

"You want me to pack it?" David asked.

"Nah, I'm used to it," Jen replied, ducking under the yoke and hauling herself up with the load balanced on her shoulders. I was duly impressed. We set off.

It was still dark, and we were the only ones out. We walked down the middle of the street, Jen handing papers off to each of us in turn, giving instructions on which houses wanted their papers tucked inside their screen doors, and which ones were okay with us just tossing them on their porches.

We were starting on the third block when we first saw the figure lying in the street. I think David saw it first, but just as he was raising his arm, Jen stopped dead, staring. The man was lying face down, next to the curb, wearing jeans and what looked like an army jacket.

I scooted closer to Jenny and whispered, "You think he's passed out drunk?"

"I don't know. I hope it's just that," she whispered back.

David was creeping across the yard of the house where he'd just deposited a newspaper. I could see his aim; he was trying to get close enough to get a good look at the man, while still keeping the hedge between them. He slowed as he got close, and peered over the barrier.

Just then the man moved, a sudden moan and a flailing of arms and he rolled over, his back to us, his face to David. It was too dark to see much of David's expression, but his body language spoke volumes. He recoiled, his feet slipping a little on the grass as he backpedaled toward the house. Jen and I, already on edge, took his cue and ran.

Jenny would have outdistanced me easily, but she was still heavily burdened with newspapers, the heavy bag banging against her, both front and back. We ran nearly in tandem, following David's path through backyards, not pausing until we were four or five houses away.

We ducked behind somebody's shed, and Jen grabbed David's arm and spun him, "What was it? What did you see?"

"His face was..." he trailed off. David's eyes were wide, his breathing heavy.

"What?" Jen pressed. I couldn't speak. I was still trying to catch my breath. Running was so not my thing.

"Bloody. His face was all torn up and bloody."

"Like he fell down?" I gasped.

David looked at us, eyes alight. "No, like he'd been chewed."

"What the hell?" Jen sputtered.

"I'm not kidding. His eye was hanging out, and his cheek was ripped and... and..." David stopped suddenly and turned, leaned over with his hands on his knees and barfed into the grass.

I felt like I might join him any minute. The only thing keeping it at bay was panic. "What should we do? Should we get your mom? Should we call the cops? There's a phone booth at the 7-11." My words were tumbling out pell-mell.

David had regained his composure while I rambled. He was standing up straight, looking around the corner of the shed. He was barely listening to me. When he turned to face us, his eyes were glittering unnaturally. "No, wait. Let's go back."

Jenny and I stared at David. My mind was whirling through a million plans for what we should do next...going back was NOT one of them. "Whaa....." I stammered.

Jenny was staring right at David as if trying to divine what he was thinking. His eyes were still wide, excited, almost feverish. I whipped my head back and forth between the two of them, mouth open, waiting for Jen to say something sensible. I didn't get my wish. Jenny nodded one sharp nod.

"If you're going, I'm going with you."

I slumped, and stared at them both, shaking my head. This wasn't the first time I'd been overruled while attempting to be sensible. It probably wouldn't be the last. I sighed. "You two are nuts."

"You don't have to…" David started.

"Oh, shut up," I retorted, taking a firmer grip on the big flashlight. "You know we stick together. Come on. Let's go."

We rounded the corner of the shed and made for the sidewalk. As we crested the little rise near the house we'd just fled from, we slowed way down, looking all around.

"He's gone," I whispered. "Is he gone?"

"I don't see him," Jen concurred.

David's head was on a swivel, checking every possible hiding place. Jen continued steadily on to the curb where the man had lain. While David was checking behind parked cars, trees, the hedge, anywhere the man could have gotten to in the few minutes we'd been gone, Jen stood staring at the street.

"What is it, what do you see?" I asked her.

"It's what I don't see. There's no blood. David?" she called softly.

"Yeah?" He darted over.

"You said he was all bloody, right?"

"Yeah, his face, his shirt, his arm, there was blood everywhere," David confirmed.

"Do you remember there being blood on the street?" Jen asked, staring down at the spot.

"Yeah! There was…" David looked down. "Blood. There was blood here. On the street. I'm absolutely sure of it! I even saw him smear it when he rolled over. What the hell?"

There was nothing. The pavement was unmarked.

"Are we sure this is the exact spot?" I asked, looking around.

"Yeah," David said, mystified. "I'm totally sure. He was right here. Ang, shine the light on it, would you?"

I aimed the big flashlight at the spot and lit it up, silently congratulating myself on keeping hold of it through the mad dash away from here just minutes before. Hell's bells, I was giving myself a big old pat on the back for making that run through backyards at all without falling or spraining an ankle. If I were in a horror movie, I'd be the one that got taken out running through the woods, tripping and falling flat on my face. It wouldn't make a particle of difference how many adventure stories I'd read or how amazing I was at cold reading sheet music, because nothing in my brain would ever matter in a survival situation if all I managed to do was trip over my own feet and die in the first five minutes of the picture.

I pushed that thought aside and concentrated on the pavement. "There has to be an explanation," I insisted.

Jenny straightened up suddenly and announced, "Probably so. And while you ponder it and more than likely figure it out, I need to get this route finished."

David, who still looked pretty amped, glanced at her. "Yeah?"

"Yeah," she said firmly. "It's my job. I have to get it done."

It was times like these when Jenny's overly-developed sense of responsibility frustrated me. I understood it, and normally I admired her for it, but there were times she seemed a little obsessive, like she couldn't ignore it even if she wanted to. I rarely felt compelled to argue with her about it, though. For one thing, it would have been pointless. Nobody won arguments with Jenny, ever. But for the most part, I took it as a challenge. She had the focus; it was my job to come up with strategies to make stuff work. David, for his part, was game for anything. He was the moral support and one half of the heavy-lifting.

Together we made a killer team.

And that morning, that was what was going to save our lives.

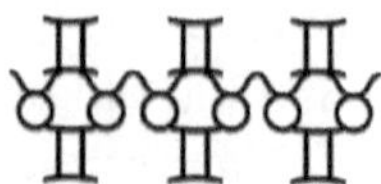

It was my idea to stick closer together than we had been before. "If we're going to finish this thing, let's do it fast. We don't know where that guy is now, what his deal is, or what ate his face. We should be careful. Jen, don't go down the middle. Stay on the side of the street where we are. David and I will stay close, and you can watch our backs."

"Good thinking, Ang," said Jen.

"Right. And keep your box cutter out and handy. I've got the flashlight. David, what have you got?" David pulled out the Swiss Army knife Mr. Rakow had given him. He'd had it for a while, but I hadn't noticed him carrying it every day until after Christmas break. I nodded, and we took off.

We raced through the next three or four blocks. There was no chitchat, no dawdling. Jen directed us. David was faster, he sometimes delivered two papers to my one. Jen's bag got emptier and emptier until we were down to the last dozen or so papers.

"David, take one each to that duplex. Angie, toss this one inside the screen porch, the door usually isn't even latched."

I looked at the house. It was a two-story, one of few amid all the ranches. The screen door hung slightly ajar. A tangle of unkempt bushes grew along the front, reaching over the stair railing. I grabbed the paper and jogged down the block.

"Almost done," I muttered to myself. "Almost done with this stupid paper route and we can go home and get some sleep." I was exhausted. Whatever rush I'd gotten from the scare had worn off with all the running around, and my lack of sleep was kicking my butt.

A few clouds had crept in and what little light the impending sunrise was offering was muted. The front steps were dark. Nervousness pricked my belly. Tiredness made me ignore it. I darted up the steps and poked the paper in through the slightly open screen door. I pivoted on the top step and started down. Out of the corner of my eye, I saw something move.

My body tried to freeze, but I was mid-step, and gravity spoke more powerfully than fear. I stumbled on the next to last step and flung my arm out to keep my balance. Something grabbed it and twisted.

The hand on my arm was cold and viciously strong. For a long, frozen moment I stared at the creature who had me. Its face was barely intact. One eye stared at me with feverish brightness, the other was mangled in the mass of blood and gore that comprised the rest of the face. A surprisingly tidy and intact ponytail lay primly over the one good shoulder, the one attached to the arm that had me. The other side, the whole left side of the creature, was crushed and bloody. Its left leg was twisted oddly, the shoe missing.

I wanted to scream, but a petrified squeak was the only sound that emerged. I fell to one knee, the thing keeping its painful grip on my arm. Terror enveloped me. A piece of useless advice I'd read in some story or other flashed through my mind. *In a fight, you have to keep your feet. If you go down, it's all over. If they start kicking you, you're dead.*

Great. That was great. Some groady freaking Creepshow lunatic was going to kill me on the sidewalk in front of a house in my own neighborhood and I was going to die recounting useless book dialog in my head. Then the thing wrenched my arm like it was trying to twist the cap off a bottle, and bright, explosive pain flashed through my brain.

I didn't respond so much as react. My body spasmed violently in an attempt to untwist my left arm. My right hand, still holding tight to the big flashlight, flew up as I twisted away, and connected with something soft. The grip on my left arm eased marginally.

That's when I saw my friends. Jenny was rushing towards me, holding the newspaper bag up in both hands like a shield. She hit the thing full speed at about chest height, on its injured side. It saw her coming at the last second and released me so it could raise its unmangled arm in a defensive gesture. That arm got tangled in the newspaper pocket of the bag, and the thing forgot about me entirely. Jen took the opportunity to shove hard and force it back.

David rushed in from behind me and tried to pull me up. When he touched my left arm, a broken sound erupted from my throat. Without losing a beat, he shifted his grip and dragged me up by my armpits. Jenny had knocked the creature, still tangled in her newspaper bag, into the overgrown bushes and was hauling ass back toward the sidewalk.

"Run! Fucking run!"

We ran. I was going flat out, my left arm clenched against my chest, every jarring step an agony. David kept pace with me on the right, and Jenny had our backs, urging us onward. My only thought was to get away as fast as possible. To that end, some vague animal part of my brain had pointed me downhill. Toward the park.

We pelted down, through yards, cutting through alleys, pain shooting in staccato bursts through my arm and brain. Jenny kept watch behind us. David attempted to route us whichever way offered the most cover until we hit the park. Hamilton Park was plenty shady, but the trees were too far apart to offer much cover. David led us around the far side of a brick picnic shelter, and we crouched, gasping for air.

I fell to my knees, tears I didn't remember crying wet on my face. David kept watch around the corner while Jenny knelt next to me.

"Are you okay, Angie? Do you think it's broken?" she whispered.

"I don't know. I've never broken anything before. It hurts bad, though. I thought when you broke a bone it stuck out from the skin?" I peered at my arm through blurry eyes.

"Not always, not if it's twisted like that." David hissed. I looked at him wonderingly. He didn't elaborate.

Jenny interrupted my hazy train of thought. "We need a plan, guys. We need to get to cover, and a phone."

"Down there," David pointed. We looked down the hill. At the bottom, across the bridge that spanned the creek, sat the municipal swimming pool. Like most every pool everywhere, it was a big rectangle, with a brick structure at one end that held the office and the changing rooms.

"How are we going to get in?" I asked, the pain was making it harder to connect the dots. "The fence goes all the way around, and the front has that metal garage door thing. What am I missing?"

David looked over my head at Jen. "Think you can still do it?" he asked.

"Yeah," she replied with certainty.

"Do what?" I asked, lost.

"Get over the fence, and open the fire door from the inside." Jen stood and reached out to help me up. "But first, we have to get down there. Any sign of that thing?"

"Not yet, but I don't think we stopped it for good. It's probably looking for us. We need to get moving," I hissed.

"Right. What's our best strategy?" Jen whispered.

"If we go straight at it, we're going to have zero cover when we cross that parking lot. If we work our way around on the north side, we'll have some protection, but we'll have to cross the bridge either way. For part of the time we'll be open targets," David muttered.

That's when we heard the dogs. Someone in the house on the corner, closest to the entrance to the park, let their dogs out. I knew that house, and those dogs. There were three of them, one little one, and two big ones. I don't think they ever got walked, I never saw them anyplace but in their yard. Mr. Rakow always said that was the best way to make a dog go crazy. These dogs were for sure crazy. Most kids, on their way to the pool, walked on the other side of the street if they were out. A few kids would taunt them, but their owner was just as mean as they were, and it was a great way to get yelled at.

They started barking that bark they used when someone was too near their fence. We'd all heard it before, but this time it sounded different. This was a louder, more panicked-sounding barrage of barks. Understanding passed between the three of us. The thing was on its way.

I took Jen's proffered hand and scrambled to my feet. "We'll be in full view if we go straight. Head for the trees!" We ran, crouched over as best we could into the trees along the north side of the park. They were mostly pines, which was good, as the branches were closer to the ground and gave better cover, but there were about half as many of them as I'd have liked. There were still wide breaks between where we'd have no concealment. We just had to move fast.

Then things got weirder. We had made it to the first

row of trees, zipped quickly through the open space and dashed on to another grouping, when the air seemed suddenly ice cold, like it was February instead of June. At first, I thought it was just me, but when we crouched to scout out the next open space, I saw goosebumps on David's arms and heard Jenny whisper, "What the hell, you guys, I can see my breath!"

Sticks crunched behind us. David shot a quick glance that direction and hissed, "Run!"

We fled like scared rabbits to the next bit of cover; four or five trees next to some playground equipment. The tree branches here didn't go all the way to the ground, so instead, we crouched behind the big barrel roller. I don't know who cooked this particular genius piece of playground equipment up. It was essentially a hamster wheel for kids, and it was awesome if you wanted huge splinters or a concussion. Fun, not so much. It did, however, offer a little bit of cover, as it was built inside a sort of shed-like construct with a roof.

We paused on the far side of it, me catching my breath, David watching all around us. The air was still freezing cold, and something just felt wrong. Badly wrong. I so desperately wanted nothing more than to be away from here, out of this mess. Home and safe. But that seemed a million miles away. I tried to clamp down on my panic and force myself to think.

"How much farther is the pool?" I hissed at Jen, peering back over my shoulder, through the giant hole in the little building that was the spinning barrel.

"It's, like, a little farther than our race route in the alley to the bridge. Then across that and up to the building." Jen said. David nodded, still scanning the area from the edge of the structure. "There are two more good spots of cover between."

"Ok, let's…" I didn't finish, because suddenly, there

it was, not ten feet away on the other side of the barrel. I was a thousand percent sure it hadn't approached from any direction at all; because I had been looking at exactly that space while Jen spoke. It just freaking appeared out of thin air.

I froze. Just completely froze. Jenny said later I turned instantly white like I was looking at a ghost, which, technically, I might have been. But if this thing was a ghost, it was no spooky see-through apparition. It was fully there and fully real.

It was covered in blood. Just like David had said earlier – its face, arm, all down one side was ripped open, and blood was everywhere. Its face did look sort of chewed, but it also looked cut and smashed. I'd never seen anybody who had gone through the windshield of a car, but I supposed it might look something like this if that person had also been crushed and somehow torn at the same time. Its left arm and leg were at broken angles, and the left shoulder was up around ear level. It had on jeans and one boot. The left boot was missing, the sock, once presumably white, was dark red with blood.

As horrible as everything I was looking at was, the face was by far and away the worst. The entire left side of the thing's face was smashed and almost unrecognizable. But the other side was somehow worse. The right side of the mouth was drawn up into a grimace, broken teeth poking through the lip and cheek. The thing's tongue hung out of the broken side of its face, like little dogs who've had a bunch of their teeth pulled.

When you see that on a little old dog, though, it's sort of pathetic and funny. This creature was neither of those. As beat to hell as this thing was, it really should have looked weak and sad, but it didn't. It looked angry. Angry and mean as hell.

The one functioning eye, the right one, was darting

all around, seeking. The right hand was fisted around something, at first glance, I couldn't tell what. It was metal, with one rounded end and one sharp, broken end.

It was on the other side of the barrel. If we moved, it was going to see us. If we didn't move, it was going to see us eventually. We were screwed either way. Jen tugged me back so my eye was no longer peeping at the thing. We stared at each other in the scant second of refuge we had left.

I needed to think. I needed to plan. I was the part of the team that was supposed to come up with the smart thing to do. My heart jackhammered. My brain shot craps. I had nothing. Nothing but an intense desire to flee.

It was David who took charge. Using hand signals we'd practiced a million times playing hide and seek, he indicated that Jenny and I were to make for the pool. He would act as the distraction. There was no time to object. Jenny pinned him for a millisecond with a silent stare that communicated volumes, hauled on my unhurt shoulder, and we ran like hell.

I tried not to look back, but when I heard the thing roar, I couldn't help myself. I had a horrifyingly clear view, framed by the square, red-roofed building that surrounded the round barrel, in turn, set off by the picturesque green trees and brightly painted playground equipment in the clearing.

I could see David's plan laid out before me clear as day. He was to going to get the barrel spinning and lure the thing inside it. If I'd been thinking, I'd have shot a million holes into the plan: you don't have time; it's too heavy for you to start by yourself; you won't get it going fast enough; the thing won't fall for it, and you'll be trapped inside the stupid-ass spinning wheel with no way to escape, and on and on.

But that was just it. I hadn't been thinking. I'd panicked, and my fabulous freaking brain had failed me. Failed David. He was going to die, and it was all my fault.

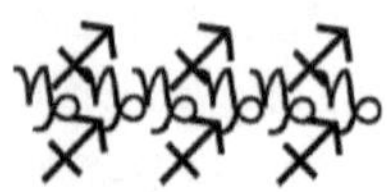

I skidded to a stop, falling to one knee. I almost dropped the flashlight in my frantic attempt to catch myself from falling on my hurt arm. Jen saw me and turned, trying to stop her forward motion and nearly falling herself.

"He can't! We have to…." I gasped.

"No, dammit, Ang, he's got this! You have to trust him!" She pulled on my shoulder, trying to get me back on my feet. Forty yards away the scene played out in front of my horrified eyes.

David had gotten the barrel going with a pull before he jumped inside and started running. These things were sort of like running on a log down a river. The faster you ran, the faster it spun. The problem, of course, was that if all the participants inside weren't running at exactly the same speed, someone would fall or get spun up the rounded inner wall and then get dumped unceremoniously on their head. There was a reason these things disappeared from playgrounds. It's a wonder anyone ever survived this stuff, spines and brains intact.

He had, at best, a few seconds to get the heavy barrel spinning before the thing reached him. Normally, two or three kids would get it rolling together. The bigger and heavier the kids, the better. It was pure physics. On any other day, it should have been impossible for him alone to make it happen.

Clearly, this was no ordinary day.

By the time we turned to look, he already had the barrel rolling fast enough that he was jogging, if a little slowly, inside it. He also had the creature's undivided attention. It was making a beeline for the barrel, as straight as it could, anyway. That twisted and broken left leg slowed it down visibly, but not nearly as much as it should have.

Seriously, there was no way anything injured that badly should have been walking. Or even breathing. It lurched forward on its intact leg, dragging the broken one along, brandishing the metal object in its right hand. Jenny's hand clenched on my shoulder. We knew we should be running, but we couldn't bring ourselves to look away.

David had started running in the center of the barrel. He would have had to, to get the most traction. As the creature moved closer from the far side, we could see him shifting slightly, coming closer to our side of the cylinder. The creature bellowed out another terrifying howl, and David responded with his own roar of challenge.

"Come and get it, you ugly creep! Come at me!"

His taunt seemed to infuriate the thing. It screamed louder and picked up speed, lurching toward him. David ran even faster, trying to get as much speed going as possible. Jenny and I held a collective breath.

David continued shouting, but I could tell he was gauging the distance carefully, edging closer and closer to the far side as the thing approached. When it launched itself off its good leg and dove at him, he was ready.

They jumped at almost exactly the same second – the creature into the barrel, David out the other side. David's plan worked almost flawlessly. Once gravity caught hold of the creature and dragged it downward out of its leap, it hit the spinning interior of the barrel and centrifugal force took over.

The creature didn't so much land as bounce inside the spinning barrel. It hit the bottom and was immediately spun up one side where it flipped and bounced again, this time landing on its broken side. The scream that ensued, magnified by the echo of the barrel, was that of a wounded animal, bereft of its prey. And the spin continued.

Jenny and I watched it, horrified. I don't know about her, but I had a sudden flashback to a news article I'd seen, about somebody's cat getting into a dryer that was accidentally turned on. It was meant to be a cautionary tale, never to leave your dryer sitting open, but the thought of it had always haunted me.

This would too.

David had timed his move precisely and there was no doubt in my mind he was athletic enough to land that jump at a full run and catch up with us handily. He'd thought it out. He'd considered the variables. It should have gone perfectly.

Except for the gear shifter. That's what that metal thing was. The kind you see in a car with a clutch. My brain identified it, just as it left the creature's hand and went spinning through the air.

As the creature vaulted into the barrel, it flung its weapon at David. The odds against that throw connecting with anything at all, given the circumstances, were so great, at first I thought there was no way. Unfortunately, fate, or the gods, or whatever was in charge of the insanity on that morning saw it differently.

The shifter spun end over end straight at David's head. It caught him mid-air, leaping from the barrel. If only the ball-shaped end had hit him, he might have ended up with a horrible bruise, maybe a mild concussion. But it didn't.

The jagged, broken end, the end that had been

ripped apart from the mechanism inside the car. That's what hit him. It caught him on the side of the head, just as he was turning away. Jenny and I flinched simultaneously. He stumbled and rolled before regaining his feet, blood dripping from the side of his face, his expression hard.

"Go! Go! Go!" he shouted at us.

We went.

We sprinted as fast as we possibly could for the bridge that connected this part of the park with the pool. Of the three of us, Jenny was the only one still unmarked, and by the time we hit the bridge she was all but pushing us along.

"Go! Get around to the fire door! I'll let you in!" she shouted. She split off, shoving us toward the side of the squat brick building while she ran for the fence that surrounded the pool itself.

"How is she going to get in there?" I gasped, running with David to the side of the building.

"There's a tree close enough. She can swing over. She's done it before."

"What? When?" I asked. "How do I not know about this?"

We'd reached the fire door, which was immediately next to the fence on the opposite side of where Jen was headed. I peeked around the edge of the building, trying to catch a glimpse of what was happening.

David leaned gasping up against the wall by the door. He wiped the blood from his cheek and swore.

"Oh God, are you okay?" I asked turning back to him. "Let me see."

"No, it's okay. I thought it hit my eye, but I think it's just … I'm fine."

I peered at him as closely as I could in the low light. It was hard to see anything. The eye was swollen shut, and blood came from a cut that was, if not in the eye, at least right up next to it.

He pushed me away, gently. "I'm fine. We snuck in here this spring when you were on vacation at your Grandma's." I was sure he was trying to distract me from worrying about his wound. It mostly worked.

"Well, damn!" I peered around the corner again. The sun still wasn't up. I was beginning to wonder if it was ever going to rise that morning. In the gray, early-morning light, I caught movement near one of the trees by the fence.

Jenny had positioned herself on one of the picnic tables that were stationed outside the fence in the shade. This one was about eight feet away from the fence, but only about three and a half feet, out and up, from an overhanging branch. The branch was, in turn, about four feet from the fence. I stared at it, trying to figure out how in the world this was going to work, and then I got it.

The setup was similar in size and distance to one of the playground structures at our school. I'd seen Jenny do this before, or most of it anyway. The fence added a pretty serious degree of difficulty. This was why they hadn't told me. I was sure of it. If I'd known they were going to try this stunt, I'd have put my foot down. It was way too dangerous.

To get to the fence, Jen was going to have to stand on the picnic table, and then jump the three-plus feet up to the overhanging branch. But that branch was too low to access the ten-foot-high fence. To make it work, she was going to have to swing herself up onto that branch, stand on top of it and from there get her hands on a second, smaller branch, even higher up. Hanging on to that smaller branch, she was going to have to swing far enough to get her feet onto the fence. Once she got her feet planted, she was going to have to get turned around and get her hands off the tree and onto the top of the fence and climb down the inside.

It was insane.

I knew she could do the initial jump, to the big branch, but hanging on to it, and then getting up onto it was going to be really hard. From there, again, I'd seen her swing that far and plant her feet, but the thing she had practiced planting her feet on at the playground was a part of the jungle gym that was considerably wider and sturdier than the tippy top of a chain link fence. I groaned.

Jenny got as much of a running start as the picnic table afforded her and jumped to the first branch. I thought all was lost when her grip faltered right there, but she had her eyes on a protrusion that I couldn't see from my angle. She adjusted her grip and then positioned herself to swing her legs up over her head to grip the branch.

I'd almost remembered to breathe when I heard the unmistakable sound of footsteps on the wooden bridge.

"Shit!" I hissed. A lot hinged on which direction he took around the building. If he went her way, and she was still hanging from that damned tree, he could take her out and we were screwed. If he came our way, we were sitting ducks. Neither option was good.

I looked around wildly for anything I could use. David was sitting on the broken step, his back up against the door. His uninjured eye was beginning to glaze over. "David, it's coming! It's on the bridge! We have to distract it so Jen can get inside!"

He shook his head a little and tried to focus on me. "What's the plan, Ang?" he whispered, sounding far away.

"How's your throwing arm?" I asked quietly.

"As long as I don't have to hit any small targets, I'm good. What am I throwing?"

I handed him a chunk of concrete from the broken

step he was sitting on. "That way," I whispered. "Toward the creek. I'll get some light flashing around down there. If you can make some noise, maybe we can get him to go down there, and away from us."

"Yeah. Good." He grabbed a couple more largish pieces from the rubble and stood up. "Say when."

"Now!" I hissed.

His first throw landed inaudibly. I aimed the light as best I could, trying to get flashes close enough to the bridge where the creature would see them, but not give away our position. David's second throw was right on. It landed with a loud splash in the creek.

I peeked around the corner. The creature had paused and was looking back over its shoulder down into the water.

"Yes! It's working. Again!" I muttered as silently as I could. David threw again, and this time luck shone on us. He managed to hit something that sounded like glass. It broke with a satisfying crunch.

I flashed light near the water, where I hoped it would be visible, and sure enough, the thing took a few staggering steps that way.

That's when we all heard the sound of a good-sized branch breaking and a muffled scream.

Jenny had gotten herself safely onto the first branch. She'd gotten her hands on the smaller one up above. The plan was three carefully timed swings to make it to the fence. She got the first one in before she felt the branch she was swinging on start to give way. She gambled and tried to make the second swing count.

Instead of getting both feet planted on the top of the fence, she only got one foot over. Then the branch broke, leaving her straddling the top of the chain links with no way to support her weight, partially pinned by the broken tree limb.

She didn't scream then. It wasn't until after she hauled the branch off her leg and realized she had a chain link stuck partly through her thigh that things got dicey. She gripped the fence with one hand, pulled as hard as she could on the stuck leg with the other, and by the time I got my head swung around to where I could see her, was flipping herself backward and down off the fence.

She fell, hard, onto the concrete deck of the pool. For a few terrifying seconds, she didn't move at all. I was pushing the words, "broken neck" out of my mind as hard as I could. "Come on, come on, come on, Jenny. Be okay. Come on!" I didn't even realize I was chanting the words aloud until David put his hand on my shoulder.

The creature had abandoned our distraction and made its way over to that side of the fence, toward the noise. Rather stupidly, it picked up the broken tree limb that had fallen on the outside of the fence. It was still looking at the branch in its hand when Jen moved.

David squeezed my shoulder, and I caught my breath, but Jen wasn't out of the woods yet. She was struggling to raise her head, and she was way too close to the creature. She was on the safe side of the fence, but by mere inches.

It crouched down near her, pushing on the fence, trying to get closer to her prone body. She had fallen on her back, her head and chest closest to the fence. I ground my teeth. She was so close to him - her face, neck, even her heart. She had to get out of there. When pushing against the fence didn't work, it tried reaching through. First with its fingers, then with sticks ripped off the fallen branch.

The first stick it shoved through was too small to do much damage. It reached her, but it was thin, and it bent. It growled and tore a larger piece off the branch. Jen was stirring, but not enough.

The creature rammed the second stick through the fence at her, but it twisted at the last second and only grazed her side. She felt that one, though, and began to struggle in earnest to get up. David and I held our breath. The thing was getting desperate. It ripped one more piece off the fallen branch, one of significant size this time. If it could reach her with that piece, it might kill her.

I couldn't stand it. David's head wound was bleeding in earnest, and he was wobbling on his feet. The thing was getting closer and closer to reaching Jen, and here I stood, not doing anything. I broke cover and ran toward the far end of the pool, closest to the diving boards. If I could distract the thing long enough for Jen to get to the fire door, she and David could call for help. David shouted at me, but I ignored him. He tried to run after me but stumbled and nearly fell.

I mimicked his approach from earlier, screaming at it, banging the flashlight along the chain links, trying to draw its attention. "Come on, you sonofabitch! Get away from her! Leave her alone you damn coward!"

My explosion of noise had an immediate effect. The creature's head whipped up and trained on me. It scented the air like a wild thing and jumped to its feet. At the same time, Jenny raised her head and yelled something I couldn't hear; I was too busy making noise of my own. But she had her head up, and that was a huge relief.

I kept banging and rattling on the fence, trying to draw it as far away from Jen as I could. I didn't want to meet up with it if I could help it, but I needed to give her enough time to get to the fire door. I cast my eyes around for any cover, anyplace I might get out of its reach if I got too far away and couldn't get back to the door in time. I couldn't climb the fence, not with this arm. I could see the street lights in the distance, but I didn't see how that was going to help me. There was no traffic at this hour, nobody to flag down for help. My only chance was to get myself inside the building ahead of the creature, but that was only going to work if Jen could get up and open the door.

I cast my eyes back and to my joy saw that she was up and moving. The thing had rounded the corner of the fence and was picking up speed along the short side, behind the diving boards.

I heard David's voice behind me. "Angie! She's almost to the door, get your ass back here!" I turned to look. Jenny was halfway across the shallow end, approaching the fire door, but she still had to make her way through the inside of the building, which was dark and a warren of counters and equipment lockers and twists and turns. She was going to need more time.

I altered my angle slightly, so I was moving away from the fence, but still toward the fire door, thinking maybe, if I cut the angle just right, I could stay close enough to the door to sprint back. A voice in my head that I'd always hated reminded me that I sucked at geometry as badly as I sucked at running and that if I got too far away from the fire door, I was done for.

I hated that voice. But it was right. I did suck at math and running. But what I didn't suck at was words. I had plenty of those in my arsenal. Maybe I should stick with my strengths. I had to do something, it was getting close.

I ducked behind the one big tree on that side of the pool and shouted, "I'm nobody! Who are you?" The thing kept coming, its weird one-sided shuffling not fast, but not slow. "Are you nobody too?" I watched it approach, keeping the tree between us and one eye on David who was still crouched on the outside of the fire door. "Then there's a pair of us – don't tell! They'd banish us, you know?" Maybe it was wishful thinking, but I thought maybe it slowed slightly.

Ok, so maybe not Dickinson. "Hey, jackass!" I shouted. The thing drew up slightly. "Ask not! What you can do for your country!" It resumed its lumbering lope toward me. I ducked behind the big oak, peeking out one side and then the other, trying not to let it see me looking back over my shoulder at David. Jen still hadn't gotten to the door.

"My Very Elderly Mother Just Shot Up North Platte!" I screeched, my voice rough and shaky. Apparently, he wasn't an astronomy buff. "Great Big Dogs Fight Animals! Every Good Bird Does Fly!" It looked up at me again and stumbled on its bad leg. *Fall down, you creep!* I thought viciously in my head, to no avail. It regained its balance and kept coming.

"Four score and seven years ago! I have a dream!" I shouted, darting out again from behind the tree, trying to draw him around to the far side. "Once upon a time, we the people, in order to form a more perfect Union! A tale told by an Idiot, full of sound and fury, signifying nothing!"

Its pace had slowed just slightly, and I thought I saw it shaking its head like there was a fly buzzing around its ear. I shot another glance over my shoulder. David had his hands on the fire door, but it was still closed, *Come on, Jenny! Come on!* I thought desperately. The thing was maybe fifteen feet from my tree. If I was going to get away, it had to be soon.

A song my mom sang popped into my head, "Passengers will please refrain!" I shouted. "From flushing toilets while the train...!" The thing shook its head again and doubled down on its pace. *Dammit!*

"I pledge allegiance!" I screeched. It slowed up suddenly. I kept on. "To the Flag!!" It came to a full stop. Unbelievably, the thing reached up, like it was trying to put its hand over its heart. "Of the United States of America!" Behind me, I heard a soft click. I tried to cover it shouting, "And to the Republic! For which it stands!"

I glanced back, and sure enough, Jen had made it to the fire door. She was pulling David inside and beckoning madly to me. I took a couple of surreptitious steps backward, keeping the tree between me and the creature. "One nation!" The thing squared its shoulders and looked up proudly, perhaps seeing some imagined flag. "Indivisible! Under God!" It shuddered slightly. I turned and sprinted.

I shouted back over my shoulder, "With Liberty and Justice for ALL!"

Two things happened. First, the creature's focus snapped back from whatever majestic Stars and Stripes it had conjured up and fixed back on me. It took off, its rambling pace suddenly frighteningly fast. The second thing that happened was I did my level best imitation of the idiot girl in the horror movies who is the first one killed.

Yep. Tripped over my own feet and went sprawling.

And, yes. You guessed it. Landed right on my broken arm.

I had never before experienced that level of pain. I expect there may be some time before my life ends that I could experience it again, but I sincerely hope not.

For the first few seconds, there was no pain at all. There was blackness, and then a brilliant fireworks show blossomed behind my eyes.

Then the pain hit.

Oh God, it hurt so bad. I wanted my mom. I wanted

to cry. I wanted to retreat into the blackness before the fireworks. I wanted OUT of my body. I really thought in that instant that I was in the worst place I'd ever be. And then the monster landed on top of me.

I froze, terrified. The creature's shred-ded, bloody face was an inch from my own. It fixed me with its one good eye, panting horrible stinking breath. Bitter bile rose in the back of my throat, and I struggled to inhale. Then it spoke.

It said my name.

No, it sang my name. "Angie.....Aaannngieee" Just like Mick Jagger.

Everything stopped. My brain stuttered and shook. It couldn't be...

Then I felt the thing grind its hips on me.

I screamed. The thing's mouth stretched into a grue-some smile. It pressed down harder on me. I twisted and flailed in absolute desperation, and my fingertips brushed cool metal.

The flashlight! It had fallen out of my hand, but it was so close...

It moaned again "...so beautiful" and opened its mouth on my neck.

The fingers of my right hand clenched around the flashlight. I couldn't swing it without slamming into my own head, so I stabbed. I stabbed at the broken part of its skull. I'm not sure what I hit in there, but it was soft. It screamed, and I flopped, like a break dancer doing the worm. The creature toppled sideways and I felt someone dragging on my arm.

It was David, pale and one-eyed, but with plenty enough strength left in those arms to drag me free. I could hear Jenny. She was holding the fire door open and yelling, "Move!! Now!!" David hauled me up by my un-broken arm and we scrambled for the door.

Jenny made just enough room for us to barrel through the doorway and then started to yank it shut. She almost made it, too.

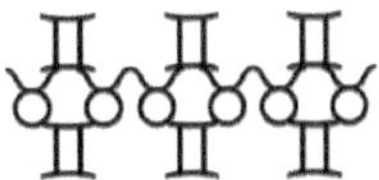

There couldn't have been more than a couple of inches of opening left when the howling, screeching, bleeding monstrosity outside got its fingers around the edge of the door. Jen had hold of the bar across the inside of it and was pulling with all her weight. It didn't seem possible that its one-handed strength would be a match for her, but somehow, it was. It was gaining on her.

"Help me you guys!!"

David struggled to his feet and lurched to Jen's side. He gripped the bar with both hands and pulled. I cast my eyes around desperately looking for some way I could help one-handed and spotted a broken piece of brick sitting to one side of the door. It had been left there to prop the door open when the pool manager stepped out to smoke.

I snatched it up with my good hand and eyed the dirty, bloody fingers curled around the door. The thing, the thing that I was pretty sure now had once been Mitch, had gotten its other hand clamped on the door frame, and was using it as leverage to keep that door from completely closing.

I aimed at that hand first. With the brick gripped convulsively in my hand, I took aim and smashed. Even I, the queen of wimpy strength and horrible hand-eye coordination, couldn't miss at this range. Pretty sure I heard bones break. We all heard the howl of fury and pain, but it didn't let go.

"Hit it again!" Jen hissed through clenched teeth. Both she and David were hauling at the door with every bit of their strength. David's face was covered with blood, and a huge bruise was already forming on the side of Jen's face where she'd hit the concrete when she fell. Her jeans were darker on one side than the other, and I realized she was bleeding from her thigh where the chain link fence had punched through. Neither one of them was going to be able to hold on much longer.

I smashed again, harder. I felt the brick crumble a little and dust flew. I ignored it and smashed the hand hanging on to the frame again and again. The thing's howls of pain and rage grew louder and more horrible, but still, it held on. One more smash and the brick shattered into unusable pieces.

My brain rocketed forward, rejecting useless ideas at the speed of fear. I needed to get…*leverage*. One of the fingers was twisted and partly broken. I grabbed at it, holding back the instant urge to barf that just touching it evoked, and wrenched that one finger back. It cracked and hung useless. The thing's scream was intense. I grabbed the next finger. This one was still gripping, but it was now hindered by the loss of the first one. I wrenched it back, and it too, cracked.

A primal scream of ferocity escaped me. I grabbed the next finger. Jen saw that it was working and risked letting go of the handle with one hand to grip the small finger on his other hand that had hold of the door. Her angle wasn't as good as mine, but she was stronger.

For a hideous second, I doubted us. Then without warning, the thing lost hold of the door and fell back. Jen and David's force pulled the door shut so fast, I barely had time to get out of the way. Almost inaudibly, amid all the screaming, the door latched closed and we were safely inside.

The Mitch thing beat furiously on the door for a minute and then subsided.

Jen's hurt leg gave way, and she slid down to the ground. David, still amped beyond pain, cast around frantically, for what I wasn't even sure. I slid to the ground next to Jen and wrapped my right arm around her. She hugged me back hard.

"The phone, where's the phone?" David lurched toward the office. It was when he ran right into a counter that it occurred to me that he could barely see. Jen and I exchanged a quick glance. She tried to rise, but couldn't get her injured leg underneath her. I jumped up and dashed to the front desk.

It was dark inside the office, but since it was open to the pool area the small amount of light from the slowly brightening sky made shapes just visible. I paused at David's side, peering into his face. The eye that was swollen shut looked worse, and he was struggling to keep the other one open. "I'm ok. Find the phone, Ang. Get us some help," he hissed. He gripped the counter to keep from falling.

I looked around frantically, trying to remember where I'd seen any of the staff on the phone. I spotted it on a desk and rushed toward it. It was an old-timey thing, with a heavy handset and the raised buttons along the bottom to press for an outside line. I snatched it up and put it to my ear. No dial tone.

I stabbed at one of the raised buttons along the bottom, one after the other. Nothing. I pounded on the hook, hoping against hope for a dial tone, an operator, anything.

Nothing.

The phones must be disconnected when the pool wasn't open. I collapsed back into the desk chair and looked back at the others, disappointment crashing across my face. We were so hosed.

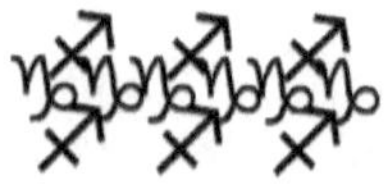

Outside, the Mitch thing was still carrying on. It was still down, and I could hear it kicking at the door. The noises that were coming from the thing were fascinating, in a horrific way. It sounded as if it was talking to itself, or possibly, talking to someone only it could hear. Moans of pain and anger were punctuated by more regular noises, noises that almost sounded like speech, but not quite.

There was a back and forth to it, almost like an adult cajoling a little kid out of a panic attack, after a tumble or a skinned knee. For a moment, it would howl and scream, and then there was a moment of calmer sound, no words, but a lower, sing-song cadence. I couldn't think what it might mean, but the base, lizard part of my brain cringed away from it in pure, crystalline fear.

"Guys, we can't call for help. We have to figure out a plan. I don't know how it could get in here, but if it does, we're screwed."

David's voice was ragged but defiant and strong. "Look around, Ang. What's in here that can be used as a weapon."

Jenny was struggling to her feet. She swayed, and leaned on the wall for a moment, but maintained her upright position. "He's right, Ang. There has to be something in here we can use."

I looked around on the desk in front of me; pencils, paper, nothing. Not even a letter opener. I started pulling drawers open. Jen was moving along the wall leading out to the pool, tossing aside floatation devices, boxes, she paused a moment and peered into a first aid kit before shoving it aside as useless. I moved to the long front counter, pulling things out from underneath. Piles of paper, clipboards, a box of whistles. I tossed things aside, muttering under my breath.

Outside, the Mitch thing had gotten to its feet and started moving. I could hear it shuffling along the fence around the outside, rattling the chain link, looking for weak spots? I swore again and sped up my search. Out of the corner of my eye, I saw Jen toss a length of nylon rope from a hook on the wall onto the desk. It looked like the same stuff they strung across the pool to indicate the deep end. I wasn't sure how that would help, but it was something anyway. I kept searching.

David was feeling his way along the wall, hands searching. Jen was tossing things aside, moving through a pile of equipment by the doorway to the pool. I had nearly reached the end of the long counter when the shape of something I'd been touching with my fingertips for the last minute finally described itself upon my brain.

Hanging below the lip of the desk, where my hand had been trailing along for the last five feet or so without realizing, was a pole. A long, wooden pole. It wasn't until I got to the end of it and felt the metal hook that I realized what it was.

I'd seen the lifeguards use it once or twice when we stayed until the very end of the day. The front of the building was protected by a metal pull-down door, like a garage door. In the morning, they unhooked it from its latch at ground level, and the springs pulled it up and out of the way. The excitement on summer mornings, hearing that door go up and rushing to be the first one inside, was often palpable.

At the end of the day though, someone would have to pull out the pole with the hook at the end, to reach high enough to grab the handle of that metal door and drag it back down. The pole was probably eight or ten feet long. The hook was metal and as big as my hand. It looked like somebody had made an attempt to make the thing less lethal by filing off the sharp point, but the hook was still dangerous looking, like something you might see in a slaughterhouse.

I grabbed at it and struggled to release it from its cradle with one arm. The pole was solid wood, and it was heavy. I swung it around victoriously to face the others. My fierce grin was met with David's who was holding a heavy metal fire extinguisher and with Jen's who was brandishing the rope in one hand, and the box cutter from her pocket in the other.

"C'mon you guys," David said with a growl. "Let's mess this asshole up."

I was staring at our tools, mentally clicking through one strategy after another. Jen glanced outside, over her shoulder. The Mitch thing had stumbled its way back around the fence and was standing by the tree Jen had climbed to get inside, staring upwards.

The sun had yet to fully appear over the horizon, but the sky was noticeably lighter. The thing out there was a ghastly mess. The left side of its face had been mangled when we first encountered it, what seemed like hours and hours ago, but had probably been about thirty minutes. I'd made it worse when I smashed at it with the big flashlight, and there were pieces hanging out of the skull now, dark pink pieces that made me feel like vomiting again.

Its left arm was twisted at a crazy angle, I wasn't sure how it could still be using it, but then again, there was no way this thing should even exist, let alone be moving with any strength. Logic had no purchase here, and I struggled to work around that. The fingers of both hands were bent out and back at crazy angles where Jen and I had wrenched them off the door. Bones protruded through the torn jeans of the left leg.

Still, it stayed on its feet. It was moving around the perimeter again, testing the fence at every point. It continued to moan and roar, occasionally muttering to itself and shaking the fence. The constant stream of sound made my stomach clench with fear.

I despaired for a long breath. This thing was beyond wrecked already, and it was still upright and on the attack. How in the holy hell were we going to stop it? And that's when the plan dropped into my head, fully fledged.

"You guys, look. This thing, I don't know if we can kill it. I mean, it's like pretty much dead already, and that hasn't put it down. But we may be able to stop it. Like, trap it. At least until help can get here, you know?"

"Ok, Angie, what's your beautiful brain got cooked up?" Jen asked.

"Do you still remember any of those knots your cousin Rory taught us when he was back on leave from the Navy last year?"

"I do," David chimed in.

"I think I do too," Jen replied.

"Ok good. Here's the plan."

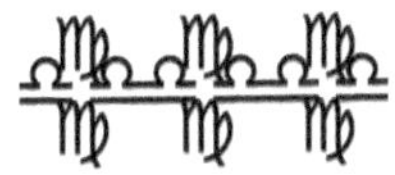

Jen used her box cutter and David's knife to saw the rope into about eight-foot lengths. After a few tries, she and David got a kind of loop snare tied at the end of a few of the lengths. They tested them to make sure they'd pull tight, and they worked. I just hoped they'd stay tight.

Jenny looked outside again, checking the thing's movements. It was still seeking a way inside the fence.

She turned back to us with a funny look on her face and asked, "I'm not crazy, right? That thing is Mitch?"

I grimaced, and I swear I could hear David's teeth grinding together. "I was pretty sure from the beginning," he said a little shakily.

"Yeah. When it was on top of me, out there," I swallowed convulsively, "it said my name. You know, the way he does."

Jen shook her head. "What the fuck?"

David wiped at his good eye, trying to clear it. "Yeah."

A fragment of a poem intruded on my thoughts, something about a 'rough beast, its hour come at last, slouches toward Bethlehem to be born.' I pushed that aside and focused on our plan, crossing my fingers that it would work.

We were all fading fast. The pain in my arm was threatening to take over all my thoughts. It was sheer force of will at that point that was keeping me focused. Jenny had lost a lot of blood, and the placement of that wound, on her thigh, had me really worried. And despite David's reassurances that that gear shifter the Mitch thing had thrown at him had missed his eye, I wasn't convinced. His face was paper white where it wasn't dark with caked blood.

Even if it didn't kill us outright, if we couldn't keep this thing contained or get some help, we were dead meat. We were in no condition to survive any kind of siege.

"It's trying to climb the tree," Jen said, glancing around.

"Let's do this," I said.

David and Jenny both had lengths of rope, and Jen carried the fire extinguisher. I had the pole in my right arm. Just as we were about to move out, I remembered the pin. "Wait, Jen."

"Yeah?"

"Pull the pin on the fire extinguisher. It won't work if it's in."

She glanced down, located it and yanked. The tiny sound of the pin clattering against the metal cannister sounded very loud. The thing that had once been Mitch heard it too and cocked its cratered head toward us. It quit trying to climb the tree and came to the fence, gripping it in broken bloody claws and rattling it like a caged beast, though we were the ones who were caged.

It roared at us, a broken and angry sound. We stood side by side in the wide doorway of the building, knowing we had to approach that thing, knowing we had to put it down or we were never going to get out of this alive. It took every drop of courage we possessed to take that first step toward the fence.

David, half blind and clinging to consciousness by brute force, strode forward. Jen growled deep in her throat and moved with him. I bit my lip so hard it bled and walked outside with my friends.

That's what we did. We stuck together.

In a low voice, I replayed the plan while we approached the fence. My voice cut underneath the inhuman screaming coming from the thing that had once been a man. "David set your snare down, I'll try to pull him into it, and if he sticks his arms through, Jen, you try to catch one with your rope. If not, try to aim him toward the other rope with the fire extinguisher."

"Are you okay with the pole, Ang?" she asked.

"Yeah. If I can catch him with the hook, I can hang on."

We reached the fence. He was just inches away. I prayed that I wouldn't barf, or pass out, and mostly, that this would work. It had to work.

"Hey, Mitch," came David's voice, suddenly light

and mocking. "You look like total shit, dude." Mitch was staring at me. I clenched the pole as hard as I could, trying to balance it with just one arm, and not drop it. It seemed to grow heavier by the second as I took in that one-eyed stare.

We split slightly apart. I moved to the right, Jen and David to the left. David kept talking, trying to draw its attention away from me. I needed to be able to get the pole through the fence and close to it before it noticed and simply grabbed it away from me. The only way to make that happen was for David and Jenny to keep its attention focused on them.

Jenny, the rope looped over her shoulder, gave a little blast with the fire extinguisher. The sudden noise made Mitch turn his head and I moved the pole closer to the fence.

David knelt, working his snare under the fence, still talking in that mocking voice. "Hey, Mitch, you miserable pile of shit, what happened to you anyway? How'd you get so messed up?" The thing growled and pinned its gaze on David's kneeling form. Jenny stood slightly in front of him, doing what she could to block Mitch's attention from the rope David was pushing under the fence. It was a long shot, thinking we could get him to step into the trap, but he would be that much easier to immobilize if he was off his feet. We had to try.

A string of bloody drool hung from one side of Mitch's mouth. He was breathing hard, nasty sounds emerging with each exhale. David kept talking. Mitch took a step toward him. I slid the hook carefully through a link that was a little over waist high and got ready.

"I bet you never knew it was me that put sand in your gas tank, did you? Idiot. Or how about those tools that kept going missing on you? Never figured that out, either, did you, you moron." Mitch gave an angry shudder and his face grew even fiercer. "Pissed on your fancy motorcycle boots, too. You thought it was Mr. Rakow's dog, didn't you? But you were too much of a pansy ass to say anything. Too scared of them, weren't you? All badass when you were up against my mom or us kids, but too much of a coward to face a grown man. Or a dog."

Mitch screamed, blood and spit flying out of his broken mouth and lunged. I took a chance and ran a few steps forward, trying to aim the hook close enough to catch hold of him so I could pin him up against the fence.

He was too fast. He passed the range of my angle and lunged at the fence, bowing it inwards. The lunge took him within an inch of the snare David had laid, but his foot didn't land inside it. Mitch's good arm came through the chain links, snapping and grabbing, trying to catch hold of David's hair. David ducked and rolled to the side, and I screamed.

True to her nature, Jen kept her head. She dropped the fire extinguisher and pulled the rope from her shoulder. She looped her snare around his arm and pulled it tight around his wrist. Mitch tried to pull his arm out, but Jen didn't let go. She walked it backward, dragging him toward the fence.

I pulled the pole back, and of course, the hook caught on the chain link, costing me valuable seconds. Mitch howled and struggled, trying to free his wrist from the snare, but Jen planted herself, nearly sitting, and held on to her end of the rope.

"Snag him, Angie! Snag him!" she shouted.

I loosed the hook from the fence and re-aimed it, getting it closer to him this time. He was flailing and screaming, and I was afraid I wouldn't be able to catch hold of him, and suddenly I had him. The hook caught him in the side. I yanked it, remembering how my grandpa had taught me to set the hook when we went fishing together, and Mitch screamed. I dragged backward, using my good arm and both legs for leverage, and between Jenny and me, we pulled and pinned him, face first, up against the fence.

Now it was up to David. He had already scrambled to his feet and was moving the rope under the fence, trying to position the snare around one of Mitch's feet. Mitch was struggling like a wild animal; it was all Jen and I could do to hold on. My hook was dug into his back and side, and Jen's snare had his wrist, but his feet were still free. He was kicking and stamping so hard, David couldn't get the rope around his leg.

"The fire extinguisher," I yelled. David dropped the rope and grabbed the extinguisher. He got it right up into Mitch's face and squeezed the trigger. Powdered chemicals blasted Mitch's eyes, mouth and throat. His screaming was suddenly silenced and he went still for a second, unable to cope with the horrible shit suddenly coating his mouth and eye. David grabbed his rope again and shoved his arm under the chain link fence, catching Mitch's right foot with the snare. He pulled his arm back, losing a chunk of skin in the process, but he had the leg snared.

By the time Mitch had caught a breath and could move again, David had looped his end of the rope twice through the chain links and was tying it off. It still wasn't enough, and we knew it. Once Mitch started struggling again, there was a chance he could break free. David needed to secure him again, either around the waist or the neck before Jenny could secure his arm.

David struggled with the next length of rope. From my angle, I could see his hand was slick with blood where he'd torn the skin shoving his arm under that fence. He was struggling to grip with that hand, too.

Mitch gave another mighty wrench then, pulling Jenny and me both forward, towards him. Jen held tight to her rope, but the pole slipped. I stumbled and nearly lost my footing. The hook came loose from his back, and he pulled away.

"Don't let him go!" I screamed at Jenny. Her face was pale and set, pain writ large in her eyes, but she didn't let go. I got my center of gravity a little lower, took a fresh grip on the pole and aimed it upwards, toward his head. I watched for my chance, he was thrashing madly, trying to get himself free, and the second I had a shot at it, I aimed my hook and yanked.

I got lucky. The hook caught him in the shoulder blade. I yanked hard and his face smashed up against the fence. David was ready. He poked his snare through the links above Mitch's head, and it dropped down around his neck like it was guided by the hand of a benevolent God. David pulled it tight and Mitch, deprived of breath, abruptly stopped moving. Snared around one foot and now the neck, my hook in his shoulder and Jen hanging on to his arm pulled at full extension, he was, for the moment, good and stuck.

As quickly as he could, David secured the knot around Mitch's neck on the inside of the fence and moved to help Jen secure her rope, keeping Mitch's arm at full extension so he couldn't move it.

I held tight, knowing they needed me, fighting the pain in my arm, in my head, knowing my friends were in as much pain as I was, knowing we didn't dare let go.

And suddenly, blissfully, the first strong rays of the sunrise burst out over the eastern horizon. If I hadn't been completely focused on Mitch's face, willing myself to not let go, I might have missed it. As it was, I was the first to see the welt appear on his exposed neck when the sun hit it.

I was the first to see the skin blister and burn. I was the first to realize that whatever demon had taken hold of

Mitch's body couldn't withstand the light of day. I was also the first to realize it wasn't going to die without one hell of a fight.

I'd thought the screaming was bad before, but when the sunlight began to burn through Mitch's bony chest, he gave voice to agony that made our ears bleed. I clenched my fist around the pole, not knowing until much later that splinters from the wood were digging horrible sharp shards into my hand.

Jenny and David, who were both still holding the rope around his arm, trying to secure the knots, were flung to the ground with the force of the creature's final throes. It tore backward against the hook in its shoulder and ripped its arm back from the fence so hard, bones and tendons cracked and separated.

The burning continued as the sun inched upwards, engulfing its chest and belly. It had tried to turn its head away, but the light was inexorable, and after a minute that seemed like a lifetime, the entire front of the creature's body was engulfed in terrible, bright flame.

As the flames increased in intensity, we couldn't help but fall back from the fence. We had to turn our eyes away, finally, from the brightness.

Mitch's burning body sagged. I dropped the pole, and the fire engulfing him burned away at our ropes until at last, the body fell to the ground outside the fence, still glowing brightly.

The three of us collapsed inside the fence, terrified but unable to move away. I don't remember how long it lasted, it couldn't have been long, no more than a few minutes, but it seemed like time had stopped.

When the brightness faded, finally, I dared to look. The thing that lay outside the fence was still glowing faintly, still vaguely man-shaped. It was a bizarre moment, sitting there. For a brief, blissful moment the pain in my arm abated, and a warmth bloomed in my chest. I didn't have any visions or hear any angelic singing or anything like that, but I do remember the smell of honeysuckle enveloping me for a moment.

Then we heard barking. I looked up to see the most welcome of sights - Mr. Rakow and Shadow bounding down the hill toward the swimming pool.

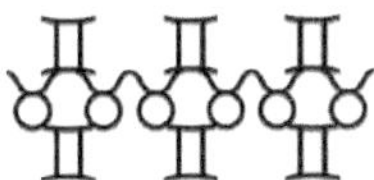

Things got a little swimmy in my head right after that. I'm pretty sure I remember hearing gunfire, David said later that Mr. Rakow emptied all six shots from the revolver he was carrying into the burnt corpse's head. He also said something about Mr. Rakow shouting and dancing, all of which I totally missed. I do, however, distinctly remember watching Shadow lift a leg and piss on the spot.

I'm not positive who ended up calling the police, maybe one of the neighbors upon hearing Mr. Rakow's gunfire, but I don't know for sure. I know by the time they arrived with the ambulance, that David had let Mr. Rakow inside the door and he had already begun treating our wounds with the first aid kit we'd run across earlier.

My folks and Jen's mom met us in the emergency room. I remember David asking where his mom was, and somebody saying she was okay, that she was there in the hospital too but couldn't come downstairs, but everything was going to be okay.

It wasn't until hours later that we found out his mom and Mitch had been in a car crash early that morning. They'd gone out and gotten liquored up, and Mitch had brushed off the bartender's warnings and had tried to drive them home.

He'd driven them into an overpass at about 75 mph. The driver's side had taken the brunt of the impact. David's mom was thrown clear. She had a shattered hip, four broken ribs, a dislocated shoulder and a concussion, and she'd already spent a couple of hours in surgery, but she was alive.

My arm was broken in about as many ways as an arm could be broken. The initial break had happened when the Mitch thing had twisted my arm. I'd compounded the break when I'd fallen on it, and then again when Mitch landed on top of me. My right hand was also bandaged; that's when I learned about the splinters gifted to me by the wooden pole. One of them had damaged a ligament and some of the fine muscles in that hand. The nurse said depending on how it healed, I may or may not have to have surgery on it. I thought briefly of the oboe I was hoping to play the next year, and offered up yet another little prayer, hoping I dared to ask one more favor of whoever might be listening.

And after today, I was pretty sure somebody was.

Someone had been at my bedside every moment since I arrived at the hospital. Either my mom, my dad or my sister was there every time I roused from my pain-pill induced doze. Jen's mom and Mr. Rakow were back and forth giving updates to my folks. Part of it I gathered then by listening, but most things were repeated over and over later on.

The fence had missed the femoral artery in Jenny's thigh, but it had done plenty of damage, just the same. In addition to the bleeding from the wound, she bled internally, which was made worse, of course, by the fact that rather than lying still and getting treatment immediately after being wounded, she got up and fought.

David's eye was the worst injury of the lot. The gear

shifter had hit his eye. By three in the afternoon when Mr. Rakow came in to check on me, they were hopeful that he wouldn't lose the eye, but it was still touch and go. While he was there, he offered to stay with me while my folks went for a quick bite to eat.

I was a little surprised they took him up on it, but I'm sure my sister's pleas for food had something to do with it. Mom reassured me they'd be back within the hour, and they took off.

Mr. Rakow pulled the chair up to the head of my bed and spoke quickly, in a low voice. "Angie, how's your pain? Are you thinking straight right now? Can we talk?"

I struggled to sit up. He jumped up and helped me with the button on the bed and adjusted my pillow. It felt good to change positions, but I didn't know how long it would last. The pain came in waves, and it was a little hard to predict.

"I'm okay right this minute," I said, "but you might want to talk fast."

"Been there, I understand. Okay, listen up, and if you get foggy, give me a sign." I nodded. "By the time the police got to the scene, there was no body."

"Wait, what? What do you mean?" I was pretty sure I'd heard him right, I just didn't understand. "Did somebody move it?"

"No, kiddo. I saw it go. Once that glow from the sunlight hitting it faded completely, it just disappeared."

"How? Why?"

"Angie, Mitch was killed in that car accident. It happened more than ten miles away from the park. That wasn't Mitch that attacked you. I mean, it was, but it wasn't."

I thought I sort of understood where he was going with this. Maybe. I squeezed my eyes shut and open again, trying to think past the pain and the drugs and focus on what he was saying.

"So you're saying, Mitch was in an accident ten miles away, and what we saw was something else. Something got hold of him, something like what, a devil? Was he possessed?"

Mr. Rakow looked pleased and patted my shoulder gently. "Yeah, something very like that."

"But Mr. Rakow, is that real? Does that actually happen outside of scary movies?" I wasn't sure how I wanted him to respond. On the one hand, it happened. I was there. It was a thousand percent real. There was nothing ghostly about that thing that attacked us, and as far as I was concerned, it was Mitch. If something took him, it didn't just take his body; it had his awful brain too. I didn't doubt it, but I didn't understand it either, and that bothered me.

"It is real. Evil is real. Not everyone understands it or truly believes it, but that doesn't make it any less real. I hate that you kids have to know it this soon, but now you do. There's no backing up from what you know, or what you did. I don't know the whole story yet, but I've been talking to David on and off as he's been able, and he's told me quite a bit of it. You should be very proud of what you did, Miss Angie."

"But, what did we do? I mean, near as I can tell, we just barely kept ourselves from getting killed."

He stared at me, grinning and shaking his head. "How old are you, Angie? Are you thirteen?"

I blinked. "Not yet. Jenny and David already had their birthdays, but mine's not until September."

"So, you're twelve years old."

"Yeah?"

"And how much battle training or experience have you had?" he asked.

"Huh?"

"Basic training, military history, tool making, weapons, strategy, or, you know, demon hunting? Any of that?"

"Um, none?" I looked at him, starting to understand where he was coming from. I smiled a little, crooked smile. "Did we really do all that stuff?"

He smiled back at me. It was sad, but it wasn't the kind of smile adults use on kids when they're trying to talk over their heads, or when they know it's about stuff the kid can't possibly understand. This was a smile between equals.

"Yeah. You did. You really did."

I took a moment to let that soak in.

"And we can't tell anybody that we did it, can we?" I asked.

Mr. Rakow's eyes shone. "You could, but if you did, they'd think you were crazy just like me."

"Well, damn. I guess we're going to need a cover story."

"You're going to need some help with that, probably," came a voice from the doorway. I peeked around Mr. Rakow to see Jen, in a wheelchair being pushed by her mom. Mr. Rakow and Lorraine shared a look that made me think they knew each other better than I'd imagined.

"Get your ass out of bed, girl," Jen commanded. "We need to go talk to David before your folks get back."

I was already swinging my feet out of the bed. "Let's go."

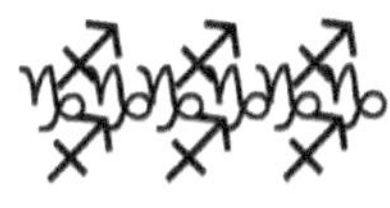

In the end, the police didn't ask a lot of questions.

They accepted our thin tale of being spooked after watching too many scary movies and being chased by a big dog. I think they took pity on us, especially after it turned out that David would finally lose his eye.

It took a while for him to get used to working around the altered vision, but he was a remarkable kid, and he's a remarkable man. He still jokes that he missed out on his true calling, to win the Heisman trophy and go on to play for the Steelers.

Our true destiny, it turned out, was one none of us anticipated, but has turned out to be amazingly fulfilling. Although Mr. Rakow was right back then, and we had accomplished an amazing feat of demon hunting with no training, it turns out that it's much safer and more straightforward to do it with good tools and a lot of practice.

But that's another story.

About the Author

Sarah Dale is an author, mom, partner, daughter, step-mom, friend, dog-walker, cat-appreciator, library book-balancer, word lover, think-thinker and picture-taker living in Lincoln, Nebraska, and just generally trying to get things done.

www.sarahdaleauthor.com

Facebook: facebook.com/wecouldbeheroesnovel/

Twitter: @sarahdaleauthor

Instagram: instagram.com/wecouldbeheroesnovel/

Goodreads: goodreads.com/stillphoenix

Amazon: amazon.com/author/stillphoenix

Other titles you might enjoy from Snowy Wings Publishing

A Haunting in Hollowfield
-Jennie K. Brown

https://www.snowywingspublishing.com/book/a-haunting-in-hollowfield/

A Touch of Magic
-Janina Franck

https://www.snowywingspublishing.com/book/a-touch-of-magic/

Different Worlds
-Lyssa Chiavari

https://www.snowywingspublishing.com/book/different-worlds/

www.ingramcontent.com/pod-product-compliance
Lightning Source LLC
Chambersburg PA
CBHW032051180726
48284CB00004B/1289